Meet The
RED
Apples

Patricia Montgomery

Archway Publishing books may be ordered through booksellers or by contacting:

Archway Publishing
1663 Liberty Drive
Bloomington, IN 47403
www.archwaypublishing.com
844-669-3957

Because of the dynamic nature of the Internet, any web addresses or links contained in this book may have changed since publication and may no longer be valid. The views expressed in this work are solely those of the author and do not necessarily reflect the views of the publisher, and the publisher hereby disclaims any responsibility for them.

Any people depicted in stock imagery provided by Getty Images are models, and such images are being used for illustrative purposes only.
Certain stock imagery © Getty Images.

ISBN: 978-1-6657-0470-0 (sc)
ISBN: 978-1-6657-0469-4 (e)

Print information available on the last page.

Archway Publishing rev. date: 7/30/2021

Here are three red apples living in a tree.

Hi. My name is Read.

Hi. My name is Every.

Hi. My name is Day.

We are The **RED** Apples.

We are friends.

Apples fall from the tree.

See the red apples fall from the tree.

RED apples have fun.

Read likes to read.

Every likes to play.

Day likes to cook.

RED apples like to do things together.

RED apples read together.

RED apples play together.

RED apples cook together.

RED apples go home.

RED apples go to bed.

RED apples read a book in bed.

Good Night

Some comprehension questions to ask about the story:

Ten Questions:

1. What are the three red apples' name?
2. What color are apples?
3. What does Read like to do?
4. What does Every like to do?
5. What does Day like to do?
6. What do all the red apples do together?
7. What shapes are the red apples?
8. How many apples that are friends?
9. The RED apples do what in the tree?
10. What word rhymes with the word red?

ABCDEFGHI

JKLMNOPQ

RSTUVWXYZ

a b c d e f g h i
j k l m n o p q
r s t u v w x y z